First published in 2012 by Child's Play (International) Ltd
Ashworth Road, Bridgemead, Swindon SN5 7YD UK

Distributed in USA by Child's Play Inc
250 Minot Avenue, Auburn, Maine 04210

Distributed in Australia by Child's Play Australia Pty Ltd
Unit 10/20 Narabang Way
Belrose, NSW 2085

ISBN 978-1-84643-493-8
L180112CPL04124938

Printed and bound in Heshan, China

1 3 5 7 9 10 8 6 4 2

A catalogue record of this book is available from the British Library

www.childs-play.com

The
Red Boat

Hannah Cumming

Posy and George stood
and looked at the big new house.

'I don't think I like it here, George,' said Posy.

'Woof!' said George.

Posy peeked over the wall.

The people next door seemed strange.

That night in her big new room,
shadows danced in the darkness.

'I don't like it here, George!' whispered Posy.

'Woof!' said George.

'What do you think my big new school will be like?' Posy asked George.

'I hope everyone will be nice. What if I don't make any new friends?'

'Woof!' said George.

'What's this poking out of the bushes?' asked Posy.
'It's a boat!   I can't remember seeing it before.'

'Woof!'
said George.

They had a lovely time.
They played pirates
and castaways.

They went fishing...

...and had a picnic.

They rescued a sinking ship...

...and they went on a round-the-world race.

They fought with monsters.

They didn't want the game to end.

'I can't sleep,' yawned Posy that night.
'Shall we go and sit in the red boat?'

'Woof!' said George.

They sat in the red boat
and looked up at the stars
in the sky.

The red boat began
to hum. Then it started
to rock gently.

'George,' said Posy.
'I think the boat
is floating in the air.'

'Woof!' said George.

They floated through the night sky,
over the ocean, and under the waves.

When they finally landed, it was very cold.

'Look at all the scary polar bears!' Posy gulped.
'What are we going to do, George?'

'Woof!' said George,
and gave her a nudge.

'Hello!' said Posy, shivering.

'Hello!' said the polar bear. 'How nice to have visitors!'

Posy peeked over the garden wall the next day.

'Woof!' said George,
and gave her a nudge.

'Hello!' said Posy, shivering.

'Hello!' replied the people over the wall.
'How nice to meet you!'

That night, Posy and George went to sit in the red boat again.
This time, it flew them up to the moon.

'I don't like it here, George,' said Posy, 'I'm scared of the dark.'

'Woof!' said George.

'Come nearer,' said a little alien from out of the darkness.
'There's nothing to be frightened of.
Let's play moon hide-and-seek!'

At bedtime the next night,
Posy felt scared of the shadows again.

'Woof!' said George,
and Posy remembered her little alien friend.

'Goodnight!' she whispered to her
friend on the moon. 'Sleep tight!'

The next night, they landed in the middle of a large plain.

'Look at all the animals staring at us!'
Posy whispered. 'I don't like it here, George!'

'Woof!' said George,
and gave her a nudge.

And in no time at all,
Posy had made a lot
of new friends.

The next morning, Posy walked to her new school by herself.
She drew a deep breath, and walked in through the gate.

Everyone was looking at her,
but Posy imagined George giving her a nudge...

...and in no time at all,
she had made a lot
of new friends!

After school, Posy and George sat in the boat,
while Posy told George all about her first day.

'I like it here, after all,' she said.
'And I think I'm going to really like school, too.'

'Woof!' said George.

That night, the boat flew Posy and George to a surprise party. Everyone they had met was there and they ate cake and sang songs together.

Posy had a wonderful time.